YEARLING BOOKS

T0155317

Since 1966, Yearling has been the leading name in classic and award-winning literature for young readers. With a wide variety of titles, Yearling paperbacks entertain, inspire, and encourage a love of reading.

VISIT

RANDOMHOUSE.COM/KIDS

TO FIND THE PERFECT BOOK, PLAY GAMES, AND MEET FAVORITE AUTHORS!

HOW BIG IS A FOOT?

OTHER YEARLING BOOKS YOU WILL ENJOY

THE BEAST IN MS. ROONEY'S ROOM, *Patricia Reilly Giff*

SNAGGLE DOODLES, *Patricia Reilly Giff*

OLIVIA SHARP: THE PRINCESS OF THE FILLMORE STREET SCHOOL
Marjorie Weinman Sharmat and Mitchell Sharmat

FRECKLE JUICE, *Judy Blume*

THE ONE IN THE MIDDLE IS THE GREEN KANGAROO
Judy Blume

THE STORIES JULIAN TELLS, *Ann Cameron*

GLORIA RISING, *Ann Cameron*

WRITTEN
AND ILLUSTRATED BY

ROLF MYLLER

HOW BIG IS A

FOOT?

A YEARLING BOOK

Published by Yearling, an imprint of Random House Children's Books
a division of Random House, Inc., New York

If you purchased this book without a cover you should be aware that this book is stolen property. It was reported as "unsold and destroyed" to the publisher and neither the author nor the publisher has received any payment for this "stripped book."

Text copyright © 1962 by Rolf Myller
Copyright renewed © 1990 by Rolf Myller

All rights reserved. No part of this book may be reproduced or transmitted in any form or by any means, electronic or mechanical, including photocopying, recording, or by any information storage and retrieval system, without the written permission of the publisher, except where permitted by law. For information address Random House Children's Books.

Yearling and the jumping horse design are registered trademarks of Random House, Inc.

Visit us on the Web! www.randomhouse.com/kids

Educators and librarians, for a variety of teaching tools, visit us at
www.randomhouse.com/teachers

ISBN: 0-440-40495-9

Reprinted by arrangement with the author

Printed in the United States of America

August 1991

64 65 66

To the wonderful metric system
without whose absence in this country
this book would not have been possible

HOW BIG IS A FOOT?

Once upon a time
there lived a King
and his wife, the Queen.

They were a happy couple
for they had everything in the World.

However . . .

when the Queen's birthday came near

the King had a problem:

What could he give to Someone

who had Everything?

The King thought

and he thought and he thought.

Until suddenly, he had an idea!

HE WOULD GIVE THE QUEEN A BED.

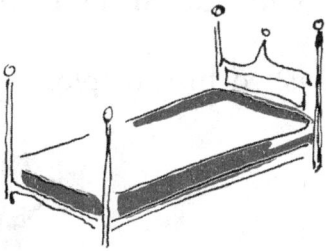

The Queen did not have a bed
because at the time
beds had not been invented.

So even Someone who had Everything—
did not have a bed.

The King called his Prime Minister

and asked him to please have a bed made.

The Prime Minister called the Chief Carpenter

and asked him to please have a bed made.

The Chief Carpenter called the apprentice

and told him to make a bed.

"How big is a bed?" asked the apprentice,

who didn't know because at the time

nobody had ever seen a bed.

"How big is a bed?"

the Carpenter asked the Prime Minister.

"A good question," said the Prime Minister.

And he asked the King,

"HOW BIG *IS* A BED?"

The King thought and

he thought and he thought.

Until suddenly he had an idea!

THE BED

MUST BE BIG ENOUGH TO FIT THE QUEEN.

The King called the Queen.

He told her to put on her new pajamas

and told her to lie on the floor.

The King took off his shoes
and with his big feet
walked carefully around the Queen.
He counted that

the bed must be
THREE FEET WIDE AND SIX FEET LONG
to be big enough to fit the Queen.

(Including the crown
which the Queen sometimes liked to wear to sleep.)

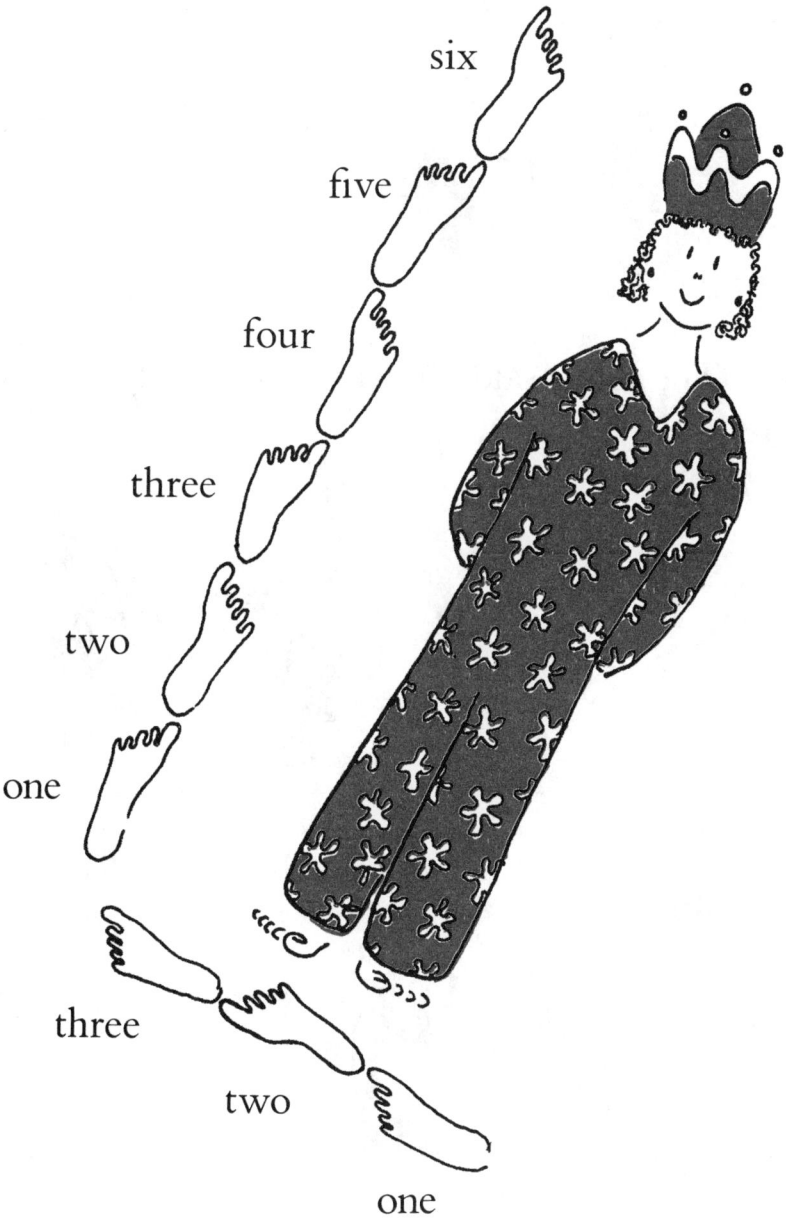
six
five
four
three
two
one
three
two
one

The King said "Thank you," to the Queen,

and told the Prime Minister,

who told the Chief Carpenter,

who told the apprentice:

"The bed must be
three feet wide and six feet long
to be big enough to fit the Queen."

(Including the crown
which she sometimes liked to wear to sleep.)

The apprentice said "Thank you,"

and took off his shoes,

and with his little feet

he measured

six feet long

and

three feet wide

and made a bed to fit the Queen.

When the King saw the bed,

he thought it was beautiful.

He could not wait for the Queen's Birthday.

Instead, he called the Queen at once
and told her to put on her new pajamas.

Then he brought out the bed
and told the Queen to try it.

BUT

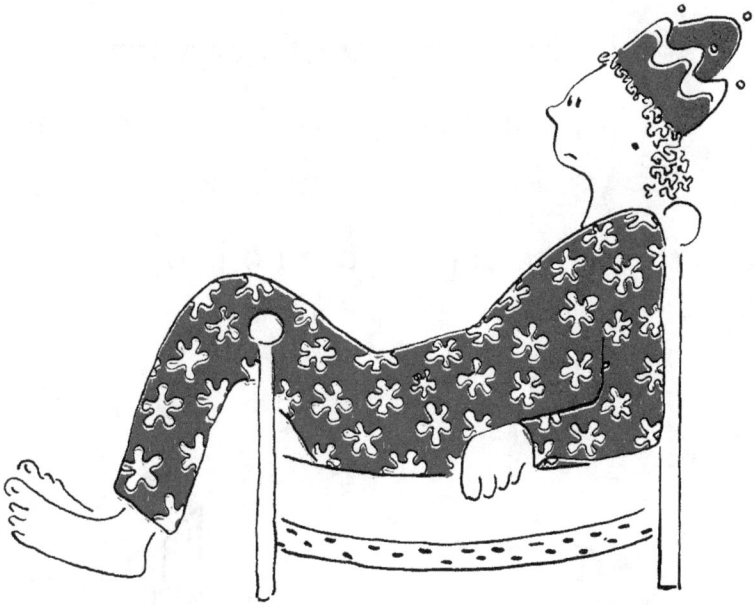

the bed was much too small for the Queen.

The King was so angry that he immediately

called the Prime Minister

who called the Chief Carpenter

who called the jailer

who threw the apprentice into jail.

The apprentice was unhappy.

WHY WAS THE BED
TOO SMALL FOR THE QUEEN?

He thought and

he thought and he thought.

Until suddenly he had an idea!

A bed that was three King's feet wide
and six King's feet long
was naturally bigger than
a bed that was three apprentice feet wide
and six apprentice feet long.

"I CAN MAKE A BED
TO FIT THE QUEEN
IF I KNOW THE SIZE
OF THE KING'S FOOT,"

he cried.

He explained this to the jailer,

who explained it to the Chief Carpenter,

who explained it to the Prime Minister,

who explained it to the King,

who was much too busy to go to the jail.

Instead, the King took off one shoe

and called a famous sculptor.

The sculptor made an exact marble copy

of the King's foot.

This was sent to the jail.

The apprentice took the marble copy of the King's foot,

and with it he measured

three feet wide

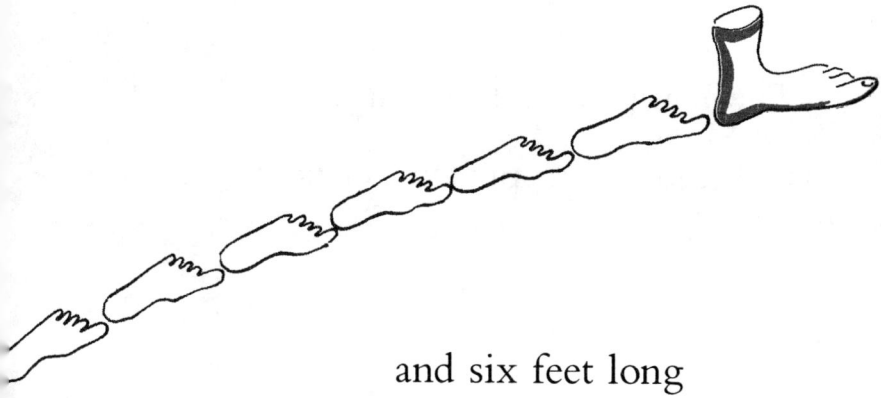

and six feet long

and built a bed to fit the Queen!

The Bed was ready just in time
for the Queen's Birthday.

The King called the Queen
and told her to put on her new pajamas.

Then he brought out the New Bed and told the Queen to try it.

The Queen got into bed and . . .

THE BED FIT THE QUEEN PERFECTLY.

(Including the crown

which she sometimes liked

to wear to sleep.)

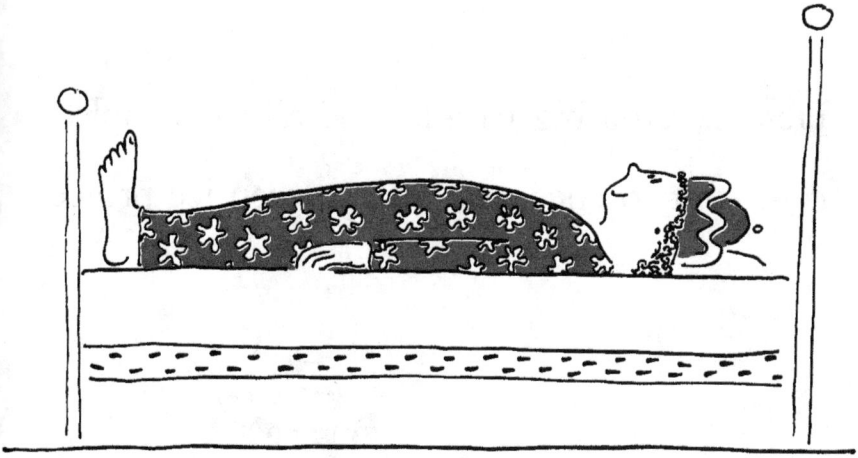

It was, without a doubt, the nicest gift that the Queen had ever received.

The King was very happy.
He immediately called the apprentice
from jail and made him a royal prince.

He ordered a big parade, and all the people
came out to cheer the little apprentice prince.

And forever after,
anyone who wanted to measure
anything
used a copy of the King's foot.

And when someone said,
"My bed is six feet long
and three feet wide,"
everyone knew exactly how big it was.